Martin Luther King Jr.

Destined to Lead

Torrey Maloof

Consultants

Regina Holland, Ed.S., *Henry County Schools*
Christina Noblet, Ed.S., *Paulding County School District*
Jennifer Troyer, *Paulding County Schools*
Michele M. Celani, M.S.Ed., *Baldwin County Public Schools*

Publishing Credits

Rachelle Cracchiolo, M.S.Ed., *Publisher*
Conni Medina, M.A.Ed., *Managing Editor*
Emily R. Smith, M.A.Ed., *Series Developer*
Diana Kenney, M.A.Ed., NBCT, *Content Director*
Torrey Maloof, *Editor*
Courtney Patterson, *Multimedia Designer*

Image Credits: Cover, p.1: AP/Corbis, NARA [Identifier: 542042]; pp.2,10 Courtesy of Boston University Marketing & Communications; pp.3,21 National Archives and Records Administration; p.5 Newark Public Library; pp.2,7 Everett Collection / Everett Collection / Superstock; p.9 LC [DIG-fsa-8a03228]; pp.11,13,18,32 Bettmann/CORBIS; pp.8,11,17,22,29 Granger, NYC; pp.13,15-16 Don Cravens/ Getty Images; p.19 Everett Collection Historical / Alamy Stock Photo; pp.25,29 Flip Schulke/CORBIS; p.26 Atlanta Journal-Constitution/AP Images; back cover: Michael Ochs Archives/Getty Images; All other images from iStock and/ or Shutterstock.

Library of Congress Cataloging-in-Publication Data

Names: Maloof, Torrey, author.
Title: Martin Luther King Jr. : destined to lead / Torrey Maloof.
Description: Huntington Beach, CA : Teacher Created Materials, [2016] |
Includes index. | Audience: Grades K to 3.?
Identifiers: LCCN 2015042498 | ISBN 9781493825592 (pbk.)
Subjects: LCSH: King, Martin Luther Jr., 1929-1968--Juvenile literature. |
African Americans--Biography--Juvenile literature. | Civil rights
workers--United States--Biography--Juvenile literature. | Civil rights
movements--United States--History--20th century--Juvenile literature. |
African Americans--Civil rights--United States--History--20th
century--Juvenile literature.
Classification: LCC E185.97.K5 M257 2016 | DDC 323.092--dc23
LC record available at http://lccn.loc.gov/2015042498

Teacher Created Materials
5301 Oceanus Drive
Huntington Beach, CA 92649-1030
http://www.tcmpub.com

ISBN 978-1-4938-2559-2

Printed by: 51497
Printed in: China

Table of Contents

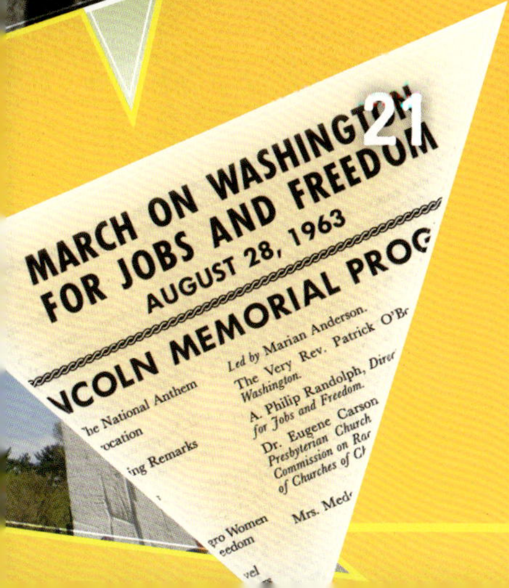

The Promise

A six-year-old boy stands in the street and cries. He watches as his friend walks away. He was just told they could no longer be friends. Why? He was black. His friend was white.

That little boy would grow up to be Dr. Martin Luther King Jr. And he would change the world!

The Young Dr. King

Martin was born in 1929. He lived in Atlanta with his family. His mother was a teacher. His father was a **minister**. Martin loved his parents dearly. They taught him to be proud. They taught him about **self-respect**.

As a child, Martin was healthy and happy. He had a paper route. He played sports. And he loved spending time with his best friend.

Martin's birth home

Alberta (mother)
Martin (father)
Jennie (grandmother)
Alfred (brother)
Christine (sister)
Martin

Students sing in a segregated school in 1941.

When young Martin started school, he learned that the world was not a fair place. He did not get to go to the same school as his white friend. He had to go to a school for black children.

At that time, white people and black people were kept separate. This was called **segregation** (seg-rih-GAY-shuhn).

It's the Law!

There were laws that kept **races** separate. They couldn't drink from the same water fountains. They couldn't go to the same restaurants or theaters. Laws about segregation were called Jim Crow Laws.

Martin did very well in school. He even skipped two grades! He finished high school at the age of 15. Then, he went to college. He studied to be a minister.

In 1952, Martin met a special lady. Her name was Coretta Scott. The two fell in love and got married.

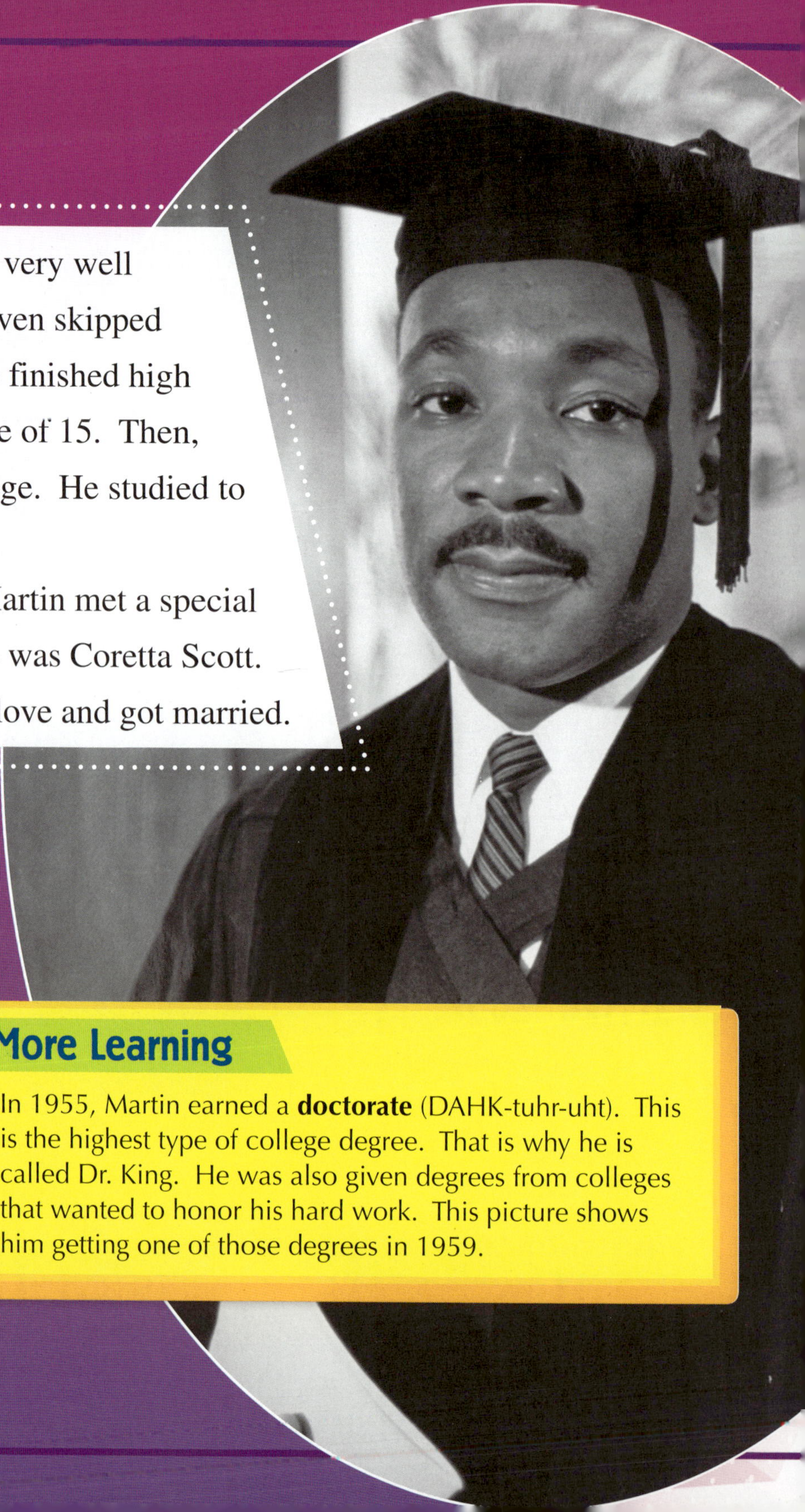

More Learning

In 1955, Martin earned a **doctorate** (DAHK-tuhr-uht). This is the highest type of college degree. That is why he is called Dr. King. He was also given degrees from colleges that wanted to honor his hard work. This picture shows him getting one of those degrees in 1959.

Martin and Coretta had four children: two boys and two girls.

Leading the Way

The Kings had been living in Boston for some time. But Martin felt he could help more people if he was in the South. So the Kings moved to Alabama.

Martin took a job as a minister. He gave speeches. He was a strong speaker. He spoke about unfair laws. He spoke about **civil rights**. Many listened. He was fast becoming a famous leader.

Martin speaks with other civil rights leaders.

Why the South?

Segregation mainly took place in the South. Martin felt that this was where he could do the most good.

Rosa Parks

One day in 1955, a woman boarded a bus. Her name was Rosa Parks. The law said she had to give up her seat if a white person needed it. She thought this was unfair. She refused to do so. The police took her to jail.

Martin wanted to support Rosa. He asked all black people to stop riding buses. This is one form of a **boycott**.

The boycott took place in Montgomery, Alabama.

Why a Boycott?

During the boycott, bus companies lost a lot of money. But they would have to change the law to end it.

The boycott worked! One year later, the law was changed. Black people now had the right to sit on buses. They did not have to give up their seats to white people.

Martin wanted to change more laws. He wanted to make the world a fairer place. For the next 12 years, he **devoted** his life to the fight for civil rights.

People board an **integrated** bus.

Martin led lots of **protests** and marches. He knew this would bring attention to the civil rights problem.

Many people did not agree with him. He was put in jail many times. But he did not give up. And he did not want others to give up. One day, he wrote a letter from jail. He told people to keep protesting. He asked them to stay peaceful. He said it would lead to change.

Police officers arrest Martin.

Sit-Ins

Many lunch counters would only serve white people. So protestors would just *sit* at the counters all day. This was called a *sit-in*.

Martin sits in jail in Birmingham, Alabama.

The Dream

In 1963, Martin led a march. It was going to be his biggest one yet. It was in Washington, DC. This is where the president lives. It is where our laws are made.

The march was to protest unfair laws. It was to tell the world that black people must be treated the same as white people. Everyone should be equal.

President Kennedy agreed with many of Martin's beliefs and invited him to the White House.

More than 250,000 people came to the march.

MARCH ON WASHINGTON FOR JOBS AND FREEDOM

AUGUST 28, 1963

LINCOLN MEMORIAL PROGRAM

1. The National Anthem — *Led by* Marian Anderson.
2. Invocation — The Very Rev. Patrick O'Boyle, *Archbishop of Washington.*
3. Opening Remarks — A. Philip Randolph, *Director March on Washington for Jobs and Freedom.*
4. Remarks — Dr. Eugene Carson Blake, *Stated Clerk, United Presbyterian Church of the U.S.A.; Vice Chairman, Commission on Race Relations of the National Council of Churches of Christ in America.*
5. Tribute to Negro Women Fighters for Freedom — Mrs. Medgar Evers
   - Daisy Bates
   - Diane Nash Bevel
   - Mrs. Medgar Evers
   - Mrs. Herbert Lee
   - Rosa Parks
   - Gloria Richardson
6. Remarks — John Lewis, *National Chairman, Student Nonviolent Coordinating Committee.*
7. Remarks — Walter Reuther, *President, United Automobile, Aerospace and Agricultural Implement Workers of America, AFL-CIO; Chairman, Industrial Union Department, AFL-CIO.*

At the march, Martin stood in front of the Lincoln **Memorial**. He gave a famous speech. It would later be known as his "I Have a Dream" speech.

In his speech, Martin spoke from his heart. He talked about his dreams. He talked about freedom and justice. It was his dream that one day all people, black and white, would be treated the same.

In His Own Words

"I have a dream that my four little children will one day live in a nation where they will not be judged by the color of their skin, but by the content of their character." —Dr. King

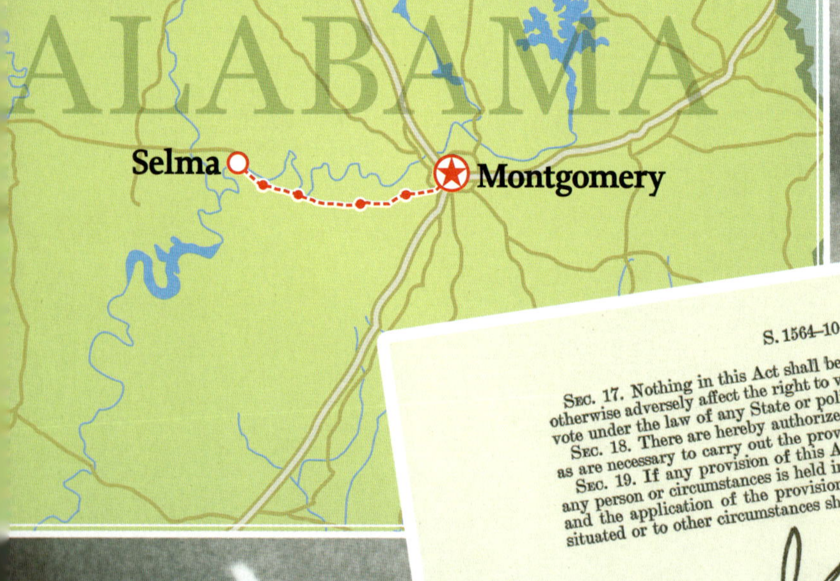

1965 Voting Rights Act

S. 1564–10

SEC. 17. Nothing in this Act shall be construed to deny, impair, or otherwise adversely affect the right to vote of any person registered to vote under the law of any State or political subdivision.

SEC. 18. There are hereby authorized to be appropriated such sums as are necessary to carry out the provisions of this Act.

SEC. 19. If any provision of this Act or the application thereof to any person or circumstances is held invalid, the remainder of the Act and the application of the provision to other persons not similarly situated or to other circumstances shall not be affected thereby.

...the House of Representatives.

Vice President of the United States and President of the Senate.

After Selma, President Johnson passed stricter laws.

It was 1965. Many laws had changed. But some towns did not follow the new laws. Black people were still treated unfairly. Some were being attacked. Martin decided to march.

The march would start in Selma. It would end in Montgomery. But the protestors were stopped on a bridge. State troopers attacked them. The violence was shown on TV. People were shocked.

The Legacy

Martin was a brave man. He led the fight for civil rights with pride and honor. Sadly, in 1968, a white man shot him. Martin died at the age of 39.

Before his death, Martin had a dream that one day all people would be treated equally. He gave his life for that dream. For that, he will be remembered as a true hero.

Martin accepts a Nobel Peace Prize in 1964.

The Martin Luther King Jr. Memorial is a 30-foot tall granite statue.

Give It!

Martin Luther King Jr. was a strong leader. He gave great speeches. His speeches inspired the young and old.

Write a speech about Martin. Write about what made him such an amazing leader. Practice your speech. Then, give it! Recite your speech to family and friends.

Glossary

boycott—to not buy, use, or participate in something as a way to protest

civil rights—the rights that every person should have

devoted—decided that something will be used for a special purpose

doctorate—the highest degree that is given by a university

integrated—allowing all types of people to be included

memorial—something that keeps alive the memory of an event or person

minister—a religious leader

protests—things said or done that show disagreement with something

races—groups of people with common ancestry

segregation—the practice of separating groups of people based on their race or religion

self-respect—respect for oneself as a human being

Index

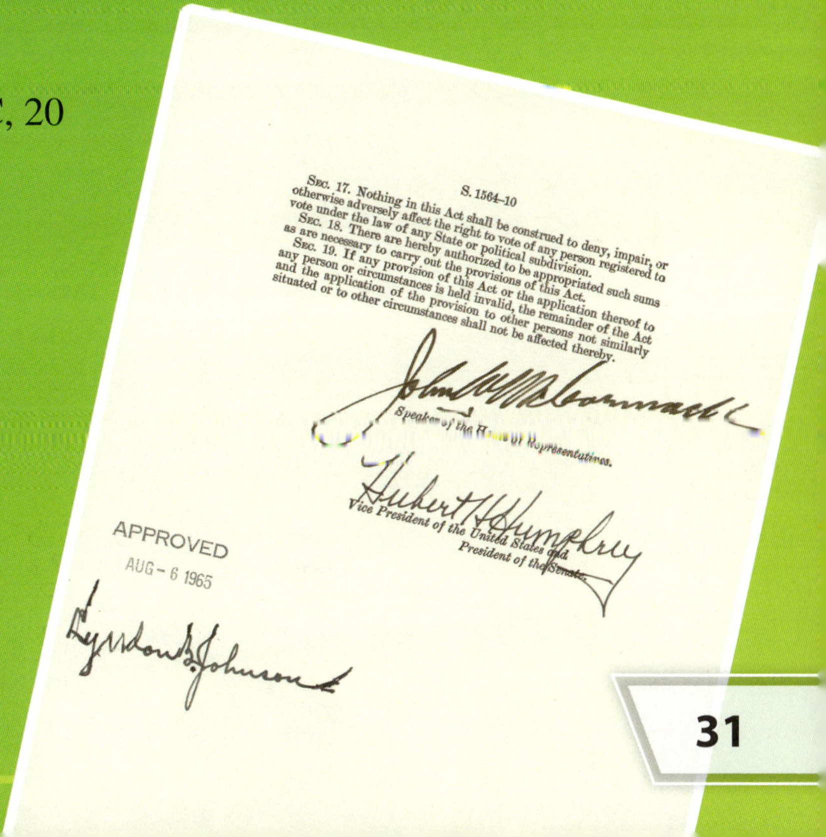

S. 1564–10

SEC. 17. Nothing in this Act shall be construed to deny, impair, or otherwise adversely affect the right to vote of any person registered to vote under the law of any State or political subdivision.

SEC. 18. There are hereby authorized to be appropriated such sums as are necessary to carry out the provisions of this Act.

SEC. 19. If any provision of this Act or the application thereof to any person or circumstances is held invalid, the remainder of the Act and the application of the provision to other persons not similarly situated or to other circumstances shall not be affected thereby.

Speaker of the House of Representatives.

Vice President of the United States and President of the Senate.

APPROVED

AUG - 6 1965

Your Turn!

Is It Fair?

Martin Luther King Jr. was arrested for breaking laws that he thought were unfair. He wrote a letter from jail. The letter encouraged people to keep working together for everyone's fair treatment. Write a letter of your own about how we can treat one another fairly. Draw a picture to go with your writing.